A Troll First-Start® Tall Tale

Pecos Bill

THE ROUGHEST, TOUGHEST, BEST

by Patsy Jensen • illustrated by Ben Mahan

Troll Associates

Pecos Bill lived at a time when the American West was still wild. At night cowboys would gather around a campfire to tell tales of the West. One of their favorite stories was about Pecos Bill, the greatest cowboy of all time.

A tall tale is an unusual story that has been exaggerated as it is retold over the years. The cowboys may have stretched the truth a bit when they spoke of Pecos Bill and his amazing feats. But the West was a big place, and it needed a special hero—someone as special as Pecos Bill.

Printed in the United States of America.

10 9 8 7 6 5 4 3 2 1

Pecos Bill was the greatest cowboy of all!

Bill was the youngest in a family of 12 children. All the children had bright stars on their right arms.

One day Bill's Ma and Pa decided to pack up their belongings and head west.

The trip went along fine until it was time to cross the Pecos River. The wagon tossed and turned in the high water. Before you know it, out bounced Little Bill.

By the time Bill's family realized he was missing, it was too dark to go looking for him.

"Don't worry," said Pa. "He's a smart little fellow. He'll figure something out."

Since Bill was lost at the Pecos River, he came to be known as Pecos Bill.

Right after Bill fell out of the wagon, he was discovered by a coyote named Grandy.

Bill did not know that coyotes were dangerous. He treated Grandy like a dog. He petted Grandy's head and scratched him behind his ears.

Grandy thought Bill was very nice, too, even if his ears were a little small.

Grandy and Bill became best friends.
Grandy taught Bill how to talk to the coyotes,
and how to howl at the moon.

Bill also learned how to make a den, how to hunt, and how to outsmart enemies. Soon Bill was as fast and as skilled as the rest of the pack.

Bill also learned to speak the languages of all the animals and birds around him. Every animal had something to teach Bill, and he was happy to learn.

But one day, a sad time came. His friend Grandy was dying.

Bill tried to help Grandy, but it was no use. The coyote had become too old and weak to lead the pack. One morning Grandy headed up to the hills. Bill never saw his friend again.

Soon after Grandy died, Bill saw a very strange sight. An odd creature on a horse was coming toward him.

Bill raced around the horse, trying to figure out the creature. All the time he ran, the creature spoke to him in a strange language.

Finally Bill stopped running and listened. That's when he heard the creature say, "Baby."

"Baby," Bill said back.

The creature got down from his horse. He rolled up his sleeve and showed Bill the star on his arm.

"I'm your brother," he said. "My name is Chuck."

Chuck taught Bill the human language. Of course, Bill was very surprised to hear that he was a human, not a coyote. Chuck told him what had happened to him when he was a baby. Bill was happy to learn that his family had been looking for him ever since.

Chuck asked Bill to come with him to his ranch. Bill knew he would miss his coyote friends, but he was curious about humans.

Bill and Chuck headed to the ranch. Chuck gave Bill some cowboy clothes. The other cowboys helped him cut his hair and clean himself up.

Then Chuck tried to show Bill how to ride a horse.

"Shucks," said Bill. "Why would I want to get on a horse? I can outrun one any day."

"But you would look more like a cowboy if you had a horse," Chuck said. "Let's go into town and get you one."

Bill just laughed. "I'll get my own horse," he said.

Bill dashed out to the open range and hopped up on a wild horse. In no time at all, the horse was tamed.

The other cowboys were amazed at the way Bill handled the horses and cattle. They soon realized that Pecos Bill was the greatest cowboy they had ever seen.

Soon Bill got himself a special horse named Lightning. No one but Bill could ride Lightning, and that suited Bill fine.

Then one day Bill met a young woman named Slue-Foot Sue. She was riding a big catfish in the river. The two fell in love, and Bill asked Sue to marry him.

Sue agreed to marry Bill on one condition. She wanted to ride Lightning.

Bill didn't think that was a good idea, but Sue insisted. So right after they got married, she hopped on Lightning's back.

Lightning bucked and bucked, but Sue held on. Then the horse bucked so hard that Sue flew into the air, clear over the moon.

Naturally Bill was sad. Each day and night he searched the sky in hopes of seeing her again.

Meanwhile, Bill had lots of other work to do. Instead of setting rope traps for stray cattle, he thought up the idea of lassoing them. Then Bill taught the other cowboys his trick.

Bill also taught the cowboys how to herd the cows to keep them from roaming. In time Bill traveled all over the country, teaching cowboys what he knew.

Then one day Bill was gone. Some say he went back to live with the coyotes. But most people believe he went off to search for Slue-Foot Sue. And if anyone could find her, it would be Pecos Bill.